KU-626-171

In the year 2065, security on the high seas is guaranteed for everyone on Earth by the World Aquanaut Security Patrol. Led by the resourceful Commander Shore, W.A.S.P. exists to combat threats to world peace.

Threats such as that posed by Titan, tyrant of the ocean bed, overlord of the inhuman Aquaphibians. He has sworn to destroy W.A.S.P.'s base at Marineville, leaving himself undisputed master of the seas.

Pride of W.A.S.P.'s futuristic fleet is Stingray, the state-of-the-art submarine. Stingray is captained by Troy Tempest who, along with his loyal first officer, Phones, is always on the alert to foil evil under the sea. And they are aided in this mission by Marina, maiden of a strange undersea race, who was Titan's slave before rescue by Troy and Phones.

Back at base, they can always count on support from Atlanta, the commander's strong-willed daughter, and other stalwarts such as Lieutenant Fischer, who mans Marineville's control tower.

Together, they form W.A.S.P.

Also available in
the STINGRAY series,
and published by Young Corgi Books:

TRAPPED IN THE DEPTHS

Forthcoming:

THE DISAPPEARING SHIPS
THE LIGHTHOUSE DWELLERS

STINGRAY

MARINEVILLE TRAITOR

Dave Morris

WASP

2

YOUNG CORGI

STINGRAY: MARINEVILLE TRAITOR
A YOUNG CORGI BOOK 0 552 52779 3

First publication in Great Britain

PRINTING HISTORY
Young Corgi edition published 1992

STINGRAY © 1992 ITC ENTERTAINMENT
GROUP LTD. LICENSED BY COPYRIGHT
PROMOTIONS LTD.

Text copyright © 1992 by Transworld Publishers Ltd.
Cover and inside artwork by Arkadia.

Conditions of Sale
1. This book is sold subject to the condition that
it shall not, by way of trade *or otherwise*, be lent,
re-sold, hired out or otherwise *circulated* without the
publisher's prior consent in any form of binding or
cover other than that in which it is published *and
without a similar condition including this condition
being imposed on the subsequent purchaser.*
2. This book is sold subject to the Standard
Conditions of Sale of Net Books and may not be
re-sold in the UK below the net price fixed by the
publishers for the book.

Set in 14/18pt Linotype New Century Schoolbook by
Phoenix Typesetting, Burley-in-Wharfedale, West
Yorkshire.

Young Corgi Books are published by Transworld
Publishers Ltd, 61-63 Uxbridge Road, Ealing,
London W5 5SA, in Australia by Transworld
Publishers (Australia) Pty. Ltd, 15-23 Helles
Avenue, Moorebank, NSW 2170, and in New
Zealand by Transworld Publishers (N.Z.) Ltd,
3 William Pickering Drive, Albany, Auckland.

Printed and bound in Great Britain by
Cox & Wyman Ltd, Reading, Berks.

MARINEVILLE TRAITOR

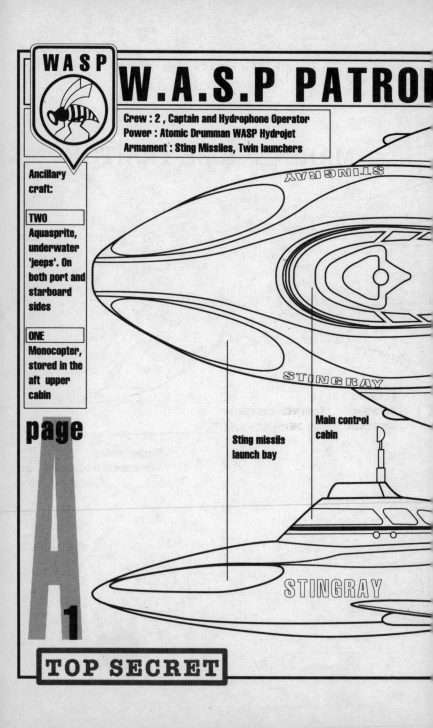

WASP

W.A.S.P PATROL

Crew : 2 , Captain and Hydrophone Operator
Power : Atomic Drumman WASP Hydrojet
Armament : Sting Missiles, Twin launchers

Ancillary craft:

TWO
Aquasprite, underwater 'jeeps'. On both port and starboard sides

ONE
Monocopter, stored in the aft upper cabin

page

A

1

STINGRAY

STINGRAY

Sting missile launch bay

Main control cabin

STINGRAY

TOP SECRET

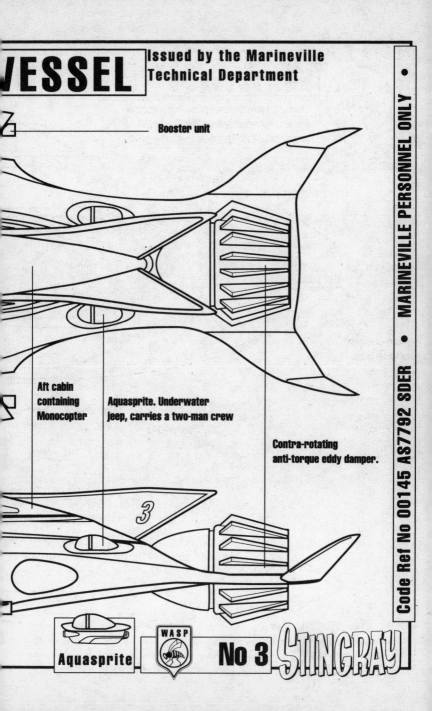

VESSEL

• MARINEVILLE PERSONNEL ONLY •

Code Ref No 00145 AS7792 SDER

Booster unit

Aft cabin
containing
Monocopter

Aquasprite. Underwater
jeep, carries a two-man crew

Contra-rotating
anti-torque eddy damper.

3

Aquasprite

WASP

No 3 STINGRAY

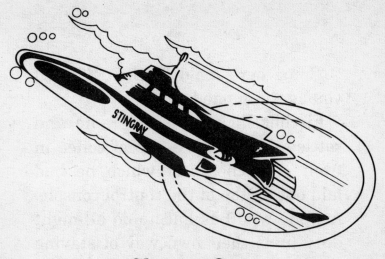

Chapter One
ENEMY ACTION

It was night-time in Marineville. Apart from the sentries making their regular patrols, hardly anyone was stirring anywhere on the base. In the control tower, Lieutenant Fischer checked the radar screens and computer displays, then put a call through to the tracking station.

'Nothing to report here,' replied the officer on duty. 'All quiet.'

'Same here,' said Fischer. 'I'll call you again in one hour.'

Fischer flicked off the radio and settled down with a cup of coffee in front of a chess set which he had laid out on top of the control console. Anyone who has had to do all-night duty finds their own way of staying awake. Fischer's was to keep his mind occupied with chess problems.

As he puzzled over the chess pieces, Fischer's gaze strayed to the new hydro-probe device standing against the rear wall of the control room. He hadn't been told much about the hydro-probe – it was top secret – but he did know it was due to be taken out and tested in Stingray the following day.

'Those guys get all the excitement!' said Fischer to himself ruefully. 'I bet Troy Tempest never had to sit up in the middle of the night guarding a piece of metal junk like that . . .'

Fischer heard a sound behind him. But he was supposed to be the only one on watch. He had time to half turn, mouth already framing a question, and then a heavy weight fell across his neck, clubbing him unconscious.

The emergency alarm shrilled through the night. Lights went on all over the base. Within minutes, Marineville was teeming with more activity than a disturbed hornets' nest.

Troy and Phones raced straight to the control tower. They were surprised to find Commander Shore was there ahead of them. He had discovered Lieutenant Fischer slumped across his chess board only minutes

before. There was no sign of the hydro-probe.

A medic was winding bandages around Fischer's head. 'Are you all right?' Troy asked him.

'I guess so, captain,' said Fischer, 'apart from this mother of all headaches.'

Atlanta came hurrying in, still in her night clothes. 'I heard the alarm,' she said. 'Father – you weren't in your bed.'

'No, Atlanta, I couldn't sleep,' said Commander Shore. 'I decided to come over to the control tower, and it's a good thing I did.'

'But what happened?' said Troy to Fischer.

'I don't know,' the lieutenant told him. 'I was slugged from behind.'

Commander Shore had been gazing out of the window, lost in thought for a moment. Now his hoverchair swivelled to face them all. 'I'll tell you what happened, Troy,' he said incisively. 'Someone stole the new hydro-probe.'

Troy was shocked. 'But that's a vital part of our long-range warning system. Who—?'

'I'll tell you who,' said the commander gruffly. 'Any one of a dozen enemies. Anyone who wanted to weaken Marineville.'

'The sentries don't report any breach in the perimeter defences,' reported Phones after calling each of the guard posts in turn. 'It must have been an inside job.'

The news hit them with sickening force, like a plunge into icy water. If the thief had not come from off the base, that meant they had a traitor in their midst!

'Organize a search throughout Marineville,' ordered Commander Shore. 'Turn the place inside-out if you have to. I want the hydro-probe found. And, moreover, I want that traitor!'

The following afternoon, despite the most diligent and thorough search, the hydro-probe was still missing. Commander Shore snatched up the

microphone from the console.

'This is the commander,' he said, loudspeakers blaring his words across the base. 'All personnel are to remain in their quarters for a further period of four hours, except for those directly involved in the search.'

He switched off the microphone and set it down. Atlanta looked across the control room at him, and saw the creases across his brow as he mulled over the problem. She knew how he must be seething inside, having to run Marineville with just the bare minimum of staff while the search continued. Her father prided himself on W.A.S.P.'s reputation for efficiency. To have the hydro-probe stolen from under their noses had obviously hurt his pride – as well as being a major cause for concern.

Then her father surprised her. He

turned his chair and, almost smiling, said: 'You had a pretty hectic night, Atlanta. Why don't you go home and catch up on some rest?'

Atlanta had never expected to hear her father give anyone time off – least of all his own daughter! 'But, father,' she protested, 'we're understaffed as it is. You need me here.'

Commander Shore shook his head. 'Honey, you're just like I was at your age: always raring to get on with the job. But since the accident that put me in this chair, I've learned the value of patience. There's a time for action, and a time when all you can do is wait. For now – until Troy comes up with some leads – we can only wait.'

'But . . .' said Atlanta.

'No arguments,' said the commander. 'You're no use to me here if you're half asleep, anyway. Head

19

on home; I'll call you if there are any developments.'

'Well,' Atlanta admitted, 'I *could* use the time to prepare dinner. Troy, Phones and Marina are coming over tonight, if you remember.'

'Yep,' said Commander Shore, his seamy face suddenly breaking out in a lopsided grin. 'That's why I mentioned it. Now go on.'

Atlanta turned at the control room door. 'If you're sure . . .?'

'I am.'

'OK,' said Atlanta. 'I'll see you later, father.'

The doors swung shut behind her, leaving Commander Shore alone in the control room.

He waited until he heard the whir of the lift, then crossed to the console. A touch on a button caused blinds to slide down over the windows,

shadowing the late afternoon sun.
Then Commander Shore sent a videophone to the tracking station: 'Myson,
this is the commander. Is the automatic message intercept working?'

Lieutenant Myson's face appeared
on the screen. 'Why, yes, commander.
It's always on. If any unauthorized
messages are transmitted on or off
the base, we'll be sure to pick them
up.'

21

Commander Shore nodded. 'That's what I thought. All right, Myson; that's all.' He flicked off the phone and the screen faded.

Commander Shore's chair glided over to the doors. He glanced out towards the elevators, satisfying himself that he was definitely alone in the tower. Then, taking his briefcase from beside the control console, he twisted a hidden catch. A section of the briefcase lid slid aside, revealing a concealed radio transmitter.

He extended the radio aerial and pressed a button on the side. 'Calling Zero Red . . .' he whispered furtively. 'This is Zero Blue calling Zero Red . . .'

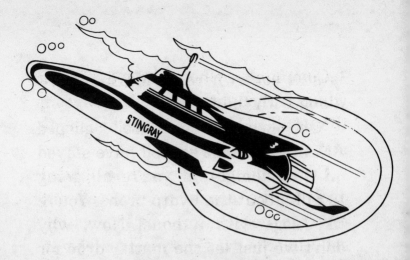

Chapter Two
SNEAK THIEF

Dinner that evening was intended to help them all put the incident out of their minds for a while and relax, but Troy could not help wondering how the thief had succeeded. 'I don't see how he could have smuggled the hydro-probe off the base,' he said.

'Or maybe he didn't,' growled the commander, chewing irritably at his cigar. 'I suspect we'll find the probe

is still somewhere in Marineville –
along with the traitor.'

'Oh, what's the use!' gasped
Atlanta. 'I might as well have stayed
on duty tonight, if you're all going
to talk about the hydro-probe. You're
like dogs with a bone! Now, why
don't we just let the matter drop for
a while? I'll put on some music . . .'

Atlanta looked for a music disc that
they all liked. It wasn't just that she
was getting bored with listening to
talk about the theft; she also knew
they would all have to be fresh and
rested the next day if they were to
have a good chance of catching the
traitor.

'OK,' she said, sliding the disc into
the hi-fi, 'I want you all to get on with
enjoying yourselves, *starting now.*'

The videophone bleeped. Weren't
they going to get *any* peace, thought

Atlanta. She hit the silence button on the hi-fi, then answered the phone. It was Lieutenant Myson at the tracking station. 'What is it, lieutenant?' she said, a little more curtly than she intended.

'Sorry to disturb you, ma'am,' said Myson, slightly taken aback by Atlanta's annoyed expression. 'I have a message for the commander.'

Commander Shore glided across the room. 'Well, lieutenant? Have the security boys found anything?'

'Er . . . not exactly, sir,' said Myson. 'It's just that . . . well, I've picked up a transmission I think you should hear, sir.'

'Well, what are you waiting for?' snapped Shore. 'Play it back.'

Myson was still hesitant. 'It's kind of personal, sir . . . Couldn't you come over to the tracking station?'

'No, I couldn't,' barked Commander Shore. 'Now give me your report.'

'Well, it's the automatic message intercept, sir,' said Myson. 'I was checking through the tape, and I found a message that was broadcast from Marineville Tower this afternoon.'

Commander Shore nodded. 'Play it back, lieutenant.'

Myson still looked unsure, but he pressed the playback button. Over the videophone, they heard a recording of two voices:

'Everything's going according to plan,' said the first voice. *'It'll be done tonight.'*

Troy and the others all looked up sharply. It sounded just like Commander Shore's voice.

'Excellent, Zero Blue,' rasped a strongly-accented voice in reply.

'*Those plans are vital if our mission is to succeed. You know what you have to do.*'

'I don't understand,' said Phones. 'What is this?'

'*Yes, but I wish there were some other way . . .*' said the voice on the tape that sounded like the commander's.

'*There isn't,*' replied the other voice. '*Do not fail, otherwise harm will come to your daughter. That is all.*'

Myson turned off the tape. 'That's the whole recording, sir,' he said.

Commander Shore nodded and took a puff on his cigar. Troy stared at him, amazed. He looked completely untroubled by what they'd heard. If anything, he was faintly amused!

'Go back to your duties, Lieutenant Myson,' said the commander in a matter-of-fact tone of voice. 'I'll deal with this myself.' He switched off the videophone.

'But, commander,' said Troy, 'what was that all about? It sounded like your voice!'

'Was someone impersonating you, sir?' asked Phones.

'No,' said Commander Shore. 'That was me on the tape, all right.'

Atlanta frowned and fumbled behind her for a chair. The shock had made her feel quite sick, and she needed to sit down. 'I don't understand . . .' she said.

'It's quite simple,' said the commander. 'I was just having a little joke at everyone's expense. And it seems you were all taken in.'

'But what about the other voice on the tape, sir?' Troy asked. 'Was that you, too?'

'Er . . . sure, that was me,' said

Commander Shore. He steered his chair over to the door. 'I think I'd better check on things at the tower. I'll see you all later.'

'How about some more music, Atlanta?' said Troy as the door closed behind the commander. He went to the window and watched Shore drive off.

'It's pretty odd, isn't it?' remarked Phones. 'I mean, it doesn't seem like the commander to play practical jokes in the middle of an emergency.'

'What are you implying, Phones?' demanded Atlanta, bristling. 'If father says it was a joke, that's good enough for me.'

'Er, sure, Atlanta,' said Phones. 'Maybe this whole business has just made me too suspicious . . .'

Lieutenant Fischer jumped like a

startled cat as the control room door swung open, but it was only Commander Shore. To hide his nervousness, Fischer snapped to attention with a rigid salute. 'Sir!' he said.

Commander Shore acknowledged the salute with a nod. 'OK, lieutenant, you're relieved. I'll take over now.'

'Oh, that's all right, sir,' said Fischer eagerly; 'I don't mind staying on. You never know: there might be more trouble like last night.'

'Meaning, I suppose, that if there is then I won't be able to handle it on my own?' Shore fixed him with a beady glare.

'Oh no, sir! I didn't mean—'

The commander's chair hummed as it glided forward. 'I'm glad to hear it, lieutenant! Now go home, and that's an order.'

Commander Shore was the sort

of man who had enough presence to intimidate someone even from a hoverchair. Fischer gulped and hastily gathered together his belongings. 'I'm on my way, sir,' he said. 'Goodnight, sir.'

Fischer was halfway home before he remembered he hadn't given Commander Shore the password for the night. Admittedly, it was unlikely that he would need it. It would be a brave sentry indeed who dared to delay the commander just because he didn't have the right password. But it was a question of procedure – the officer on duty in Marineville Tower was *always* supposed to be told the password.

Fischer glanced at his watch. He could be back at the Tower in fifteen minutes. After a moment's thought, Fischer turned and retraced his steps.

He was anxious to please – and to show the commander that the blow to his head hadn't affected his customary attention to duty.

Glancing up as he approached the Tower, Fischer saw the lights of the control room burning against the night sky. He hoped the commander wouldn't chew him out too badly for his oversight. Quickening his step, Fischer saluted the sentry on duty in the lobby and hurried over to the lifts.

Fischer sensed something wrong the instant the lift door opened. Then he realized what it was: the absolute silence. Normally when the commander was on duty, there was a continual hum from his hoverchair as he restlessly prowled to and fro. On instinct, Fischer drew his gun and gingerly pushed the control room door open.

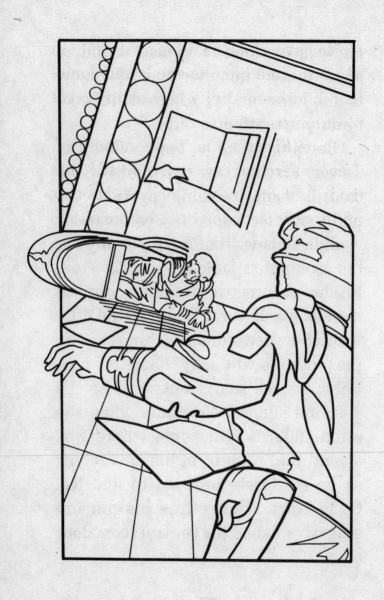

He gave a gasp. The security safe in the wall had been opened, and someone had been through the top secret documents inside.

Then Fischer saw the commander. His hoverchair was on its side, his body half slumped out of it. As Fischer approached, he gave a groan and his eyelids fluttered open. 'Lieutenant...' he groaned. 'What happened?'

'I'm not sure, sir,' said Fischer, holstering his gun, 'but I think the traitor's struck again!'

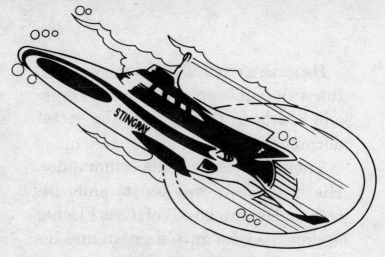

Chapter Three
SETTING TRAPS

By the time Troy and the others arrived on the scene, the control tower was swarming with security guards. Commander Shore was wincing as he ran his hand over the back of his head, but he dismissed the medic who tried to treat him. 'I've suffered worse than this and not needed a plaster!' he snarled.

The security chief, Lieutenant Brady, came over. 'What's missing?' said Troy.

Brady glanced back at the open safe. 'The top secret plans detailing how to operate the hydro-probe. I suppose the thief realized he wouldn't be able to use the hydro-probe without them.'

'That's just great!' growled Commander Shore. 'Now we have a double theft to worry about. If only I'd seen the man's face – but he hit me from behind . . .'

'Let Troy deal with it for now, father,' said Atlanta. 'After that knock on the head, you need to lie down.'

'I don't have time for that, Atlanta,' said the commander. 'There are things to do.'

'Yes,' said Atlanta firmly, 'and you

won't be able to do them if you collapse. I really think you should go home and rest.'

Commander Shore shrugged. 'Oh, I guess you're right.'

Troy walked with him to the lifts. 'It's a nasty business, this,' he said. 'A traitor in W.A.S.P., I mean. What makes a man turn traitor, I wonder?'

'Any one of a number of things, Troy,' said the commander. 'Money

for instance, or politics . . . or love.'

'Love?' said Troy.

'Uh-huh. Love of your family and friends; concern that no harm comes to them. Threats can make even a good man turn traitor.'

'Yes,' said Troy, 'I see . . .'

'Here's the lift,' said Commander Shore. He steered his chair inside and turned to face Troy as the door slid shut. 'Goodnight Troy. I'll see you in the morning.'

Troy returned to the control room with a heavy heart. He could no longer ignore the suspicions that had been gnawing at him for the last few hours.

The security team were just leaving. They had not been able to find any fingerprints that did not match with regular Tower personnel. 'And

they say there's no record of anyone entering the Tower after father,'
Atlanta told him.

Phones came over. 'I don't get it,' he
said. 'In that case, how did the guy
who slugged the commander get in?'

'Maybe he didn't,' said Troy.

Atlanta gave him a sharp look.
'What do you mean?' she demanded.

Troy rubbed his chin. 'Well . . . it's a
bit difficult to say this to you, Atlanta,
but I think your father is more involved in all this than he's letting on.'

'Do you mean he knows something
we don't?' asked Phones.

Good old Phones, thought Troy – so
loyal and honest himself that he could
never suspect dishonesty in someone
else. He said: 'No, it's more than that,
Phones . . .'

'What Troy's reluctant to say,
Phones,' said Atlanta angrily, 'is that

he thinks my father's the traitor! That's it, isn't it, Troy?'

'Atlanta,' said Troy, reaching out to reassure her, 'I'm only looking at the facts . . .'

She brushed his hand away and stood with arms folded, fire in her eyes. 'What facts? Tell me *one thing* that points to my father's guilt.'

Troy sighed. 'OK, first of all there's the recording that Myson picked up on the automatic intercept. Do you really think the commander was joking? That isn't his sense of humour at all.'

'That's pretty flimsy evidence,' retorted Atlanta.

Troy nodded. 'On its own it would be, but there's more. Like tonight – security didn't see anyone else come up here, and yet your father says someone hit him from behind.'

Atlanta hesitated; the same problem had been bothering her. 'But his head . . .' she said, 'he was hurt . . . in pain . . .'

'So he *said*,' Troy pointed out, 'but he wouldn't let the medic have a look.'

Atlanta stared miserably at the floor. She didn't want Troy and Phones to see there were tears in her eyes. 'I can't believe it,' she said. 'Not my father . . .'

Troy hated having to press Atlanta, but it was important to make her see the weight of the evidence. 'How about last night?' he persisted. 'It was convenient that the commander was the first on the scene after the hydro-probe was stolen. He told us he'd decided to go on duty early.'

'But that's not unusual for the commander,' said Phones, 'if he isn't able to get to sleep.'

'*If* he couldn't sleep, *if* he was joking, *if* he was slugged.' Troy shook his head. 'There are too many "ifs".'

'Oh, Troy,' sobbed Atlanta, 'what are we going to do? We've got to stop father – someone must be forcing him to do these terrible things . . . Help him somehow.'

'I'll do my best, Atlanta,' said Troy; 'you know that. But we also have to recover the hydro-probe and the plans. Until we have more evidence, I suggest we all keep a close watch on the commander.'

About noon the next day, Commander Shore was alone in the control room. He glanced around him and nodded, allowing himself a faint smile. Everything was going as he had planned.

Commander Shore put through a call to security. 'I do not want to be disturbed for the next ten minutes,' he told them. 'See that nobody is allowed up here without my authorization.'

Next he lowered the blinds, as before, and extracted the hidden radio from his briefcase. 'Come in, Zero Red,' he said. 'This is Zero Blue . . .'

'I read you, Zero Blue,' rasped a sinister voice from the radio. 'What have you to report? Were you successful?'

'Yes,' replied Commander Shore, 'everything went smoothly. However, although the others haven't said anything, I think their suspicions are aroused. I'll have to tread carefully. Zero Blue out.'

The door opened. Commander Shore looked up, and found himself looking into the barrel of a gun. It was Troy – and behind him were Phones and Atlanta.

'What is this?' snarled Commander Shore. 'I gave orders I wasn't to be disturbed.' He pushed the radio back into his briefcase.

'I'm sorry, commander, but I overheard everything,' said Troy. 'I'll have to take that radio transmitter as evidence. I'm putting you under arrest – on a charge of treason.'

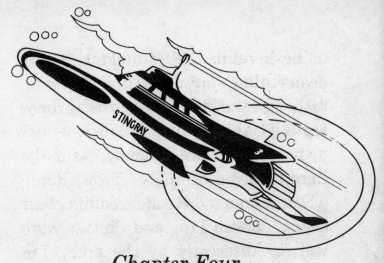

Chapter Four
TRUE COLOURS

Commander Shore nodded. 'Don't worry, I won't give you any trouble.'

'I'm afraid I'm going to have to put you in a detention cell, sir,' said Troy.

'Oh, no, Troy!' gasped Atlanta. 'Couldn't he just come home with me? I'll look after him.' She ran to her father's side and put a protective arm around his shoulders.

Troy winced. The fact that he was

doing his duty didn't make this any easier. 'I'm sorry, Atlanta,' he said, 'but I have to follow the proper regulations.'

'It's OK, Atlanta, honey,' said the commander soothingly. 'Troy's doing what he has to.' He steered his chair over to where Troy and Phones were waiting discreetly by the door. 'I'm ready, captain.'

'Thank you, sir,' said Troy. 'I appreciate the dignified way you're handling this – it's a nasty enough situation, without making it any worse.'

'I agree,' said the commander. 'You're a credit to the service, captain.'

Troy couldn't muster even a faint smile. When he saw the tragic look on Atlanta's face, it made him feel *he* was the one guilty of betrayal.

Phones stepped forward. 'I'll escort you to the detention cells, sir,' he said to the commander. 'If you'll come this way . . .'

There was a sick feeling in the pit of Troy's stomach. Even though he'd been the one to see where the evidence pointed, he could still hardly believe it was true. Like everyone in W.A.S.P., he had always respected Commander Shore for his dedication and devotion to duty. It was almost impossible to accept he was a traitor . . .

Troy forced these thoughts from his mind. There were still many things he had to do. He put through a call to Lieutenant Myson at the tracking station. 'This is Captain Tempest,' he said. 'I've relieved Commander Shore of command and am now taking charge of Marineville. Advise the airfield I'll be needing

a helijet to take me to World Security HQ. Have it ready in fifteen minutes.'

As soon as Troy arrived at World Security Patrol HQ, he was shown straight in to the office of General Fennell, the chief-of-staff.

'It's a bad business, captain,' said the general once he'd heard Troy's report. 'But you must set your mind at rest on one point: you've done the right thing.'

'Yes, sir,' said Troy without emotion. The general's commendation gave him no pleasure. 'If I may make a suggestion, sir? I think the court-martial should proceed without delay. Commander Shore shouldn't be kept languishing in a cell.'

'You show remarkable loyalty towards a traitor, captain,' said the general.

'The charges against the commander have yet to be proved, sir,' Troy reminded him stiffly. 'Also, whatever he may be now, he has served the world valiantly in the past.'

'I agree,' said General Fennell. 'That's what makes his crime all the more serious. Return to Marineville, captain. I'll make the arrangements for Shore's trial; you concentrate on getting back the missing hydro-probe.'

'Yes, sir.' Troy saluted, spun on his heel, and marched out.

As soon as he could find a videophone, he put through a call to Marineville Tower. 'I'll be flying straight back,' he told Phones.

'OK, Troy,' said Phones. 'How did it go with the chief?'

'As you'd expect,' said Troy. 'I feel like Judas. And *don't* tell me I've done what I had to, Phones; I'm sick of hearing it.'

'Well . . .' said Phones, 'you had to do something. Imagine the commander turning traitor like that – of all people.'

Troy sighed. 'Yeah. He didn't say a great deal, but I think he did it because someone was threatening Atlanta. He even hinted as much to me last night – almost as though he *wanted* to be caught. Still, no sense in brooding over it. I'll see you when I get back, Phones.'

Troy flicked off the videophone. Phones's image vanished, to be replaced by the fading blue glow of the screen.

Troy frowned. There was *something* still nagging at the back of his mind. But what . . .? He couldn't quite put his finger on it, but Troy's every instinct told him there was more trouble yet to come.

Some time later, as Commander Shore sat brooding in his cell, there was the sound of a key in the lock. Commander Shore rotated his chair and saw Lieutenant Myson standing in the open doorway.

'What is this, lieutenant?' demanded Shore. 'Am I being released?'

Myson chuckled. 'Well, you're certainly getting out of here, commander – but it's more what you'd call a jailbreak, I think. We'd better get a move on; I've slugged the guard, but he'll come round in a few minutes.'

Shore stared back at him. He didn't seem in any hurry to escape. 'So *you're* the one who stole the hydro-probe,' he said.

'Yes,' said Myson, 'and now you've got the top secret plans. Apparently we're on the same side, though I'd never have suspected it. I thought I was working alone here. Our underwater friends chose a good spy in you.'

'We might have to shoot our way out,' said Commander Shore. 'You'd better give me your gun, and you can take the guard's gun as we leave.'

Myson thought about this and nodded. 'I hope you're not afraid to use it,' he said, handing it over.

'I certainly am not!' said the commander with sudden vehemence. He pointed the gun straight at Myson. 'The game's up, traitor. You're under arrest.'

Myson's jaw dropped in astonishment. 'Eh?' he gasped. 'But I thought . . .'

'You thought just what I wanted you to think, Myson,' said the commander. 'Now, put your hands up.'

Myson started to do as he was told, but then suddenly he lashed out with his foot, planting a powerful kick on the base of the commander's hoverchair. The hoverchair careened back and collided with the wall, the impact jerking the gun out of

Commander Shore's hand. It skidded across the floor and Myson snatched it up.

'Huh!' said Myson, grinning in relief. He pointed the gun at Commander Shore. 'If not for that buggy of yours, I'd have been for the high jump.'

Shore gritted his teeth. If he had the use of his legs, he would have leapt at Myson and tried to wrest the gun away. But his hoverchair would not be fast enough for that. 'One way or another, you'll end up in front of the firing squad, Myson,' he said.

'You forget, commander,' said Myson: 'I'm the one holding the gun now. It looks as if you won't be leaving this cell, after all. But before I shoot you, I want to know what all this double-dealing's been about.'

'Headquarters and I knew a traitor was passing secrets out of Marineville,' said Commander Shore. 'We had to lay a trap to catch you. What better way than to pretend there was *another* traitor – a person really high up, with access to the top secret plans you wanted.'

'Quite a plan,' admitted Myson. 'You had all Marineville fooled. Even Tempest and your own daughter figured you for a spy.'

'That was the hardest part, deceiving them. I couldn't tell anybody the truth.'

Myson gave a bark of cold laughter. 'Too bad you'll never live to tell the story . . .' He began to squeeze the trigger.

A shot rang out. But, instead of the commander, it was Myson who was

shot. The bullet tore into his hand and he gave a shriek of pain, dropping the gun.

Troy was standing in the doorway of the cell. A curl of smoke was rising from the gun in his hand.

'Troy!' said Commander Shore. 'You got here in the nick of time.'

'But how . . .?' groaned Myson, wincing in pain as he cradled his

ed hand. 'How did you know to
ne here . . .?'

'It's simple, Myson,' explained
Commander Shore. 'As soon as you
showed up at my cell door, I pushed
the communicator button on my
hoverchair. It relayed everything we
said directly to the control tower.'

'We heard everything,' said Troy,
nodding, 'and I rushed straight over.'

Phones and Atlanta came rushing
in. 'You'd better find a medic for this
traitor,' the commander told them. 'It
wouldn't do for him to bleed to death
before his court-martial.'

As Phones went to fetch a medic,
Myson slumped wearily in the corner
of the cell. 'But who was your con-
tact?' he asked. 'I intercepted that
message to Zero Red myself . . .'

Commander Shore grinned. '"Zero

Red" was in fact General Fennell himself. He was in on the plan, of course. Too bad you didn't know that the general is good at imitating alien accents.'

The commander steered his hover-chair out of the cell and Troy locked Myson inside.

'Oh, father,' said Atlanta, hugging him, 'it's such a relief to know you're not a traitor, after all.'

'I second that, sir!' said Troy, smiling for the first time since he took command of Marineville.

'Anybody would think you didn't like being in charge, Troy,' said Commander Shore.

'It was the worst few hours of my life,' said Troy with feeling, 'and now I'm surrendering command back to you.'

'Fine,' said Commander Shore. 'In that case, what are we all hanging around here for? There's work to be done. Marineville won't run itself, you know!'

THE END

STINGRAY TITLES AVAILABLE FROM YOUNG CORGI

THE PRICES SHOWN BELOW WERE CORRECT AT THE TIME OF GOING TO PRESS. HOWEVER TRANSWORLD PUBLISHERS RESERVE THE RIGHT TO SHOW NEW RETAIL PRICES ON COVERS WHICH MAY DIFFER FROM THOSE PREVIOUSLY ADVERTISED IN THE TEXT OR ELSEWHERE.

❒ 0 552 527785 **STINGRAY: TRAPPED IN THE DEPTHS**
Dave Morris £2.50
❒ 0 552 527793 **STINGRAY: MARINEVILLE TRAITOR**
Dave Morris £2.50

Coming soon:

❒ 0 552 527807 **STINGRAY: THE DISAPPEARING SHIPS**
Dave Morris £2.50
❒ 0 552 527815 **STINGRAY: THE LIGHTHOUSE DWELLERS**
Dave Morris £2.50

All Young Corgi Books are available at your bookshop or newsagent, or can be ordered from the following address:

Transworld Publishers
Cash Sales Department
P.O. Box 11, Falmouth, Cornwall TR10 9EN

Please send a cheque or postal order (no currency) and allow £1.00 for postage and packing for one book, an additional 50p for a second book, and an additional 30p for each subsequent book ordered to a maximum charge of £3.00 if ordering seven or more books.

Overseas customers, including Eire, please allow £2.00 for postage and packing for the first book, an additional £1.00 for a second book, and an additional 50p for each subsequent title ordered.

NAME (Block letters) ....

ADDRESS...

....